STRAY DOG

STRAY DOG

Gareth O'Callaghan

BBC
LARGE
PRINT

First published in 2004 by
New Island
This Large Print edition published
2010 by BBC Audiobooks by
arrangement with
New Island

ISBN 978 1 405 62297 4

British Library Cataloguing in Publication Data available

Printed and bound in Great Britain by
CPI Antony Rowe, Chippenham and Eastbourne

I loved him more than life itself. I often heard people say that about someone they had lost. But I never understood how anyone could love another person so much. Now I can. It's been three months since I lost John. And, yes, I know now that he was everything to me. With each day that passes, I realise that more and more.

We sat close together and held hands the afternoon the doctor gave us the awful news. John's cancer had gone too far for us to have any hope. He had less than a month to live, if he was lucky.

He lived for six months, which meant we were both lucky. It also marked the start of an amazing journey, which I now know has given me the strength and understanding I need to carry on. It is a journey that has given me more hope than I could ever have imagined.

We sat in heavy traffic that evening on the way home from the hospital. We took turns to hide our tears. I tried to hide my shock and disbelief. John reached across and squeezed my hand. He said, 'It'll be OK.'

I couldn't believe he'd just said that. 'What the hell do you mean "it will be OK"?' I felt sick. My heart pounded. I wanted to scream at him for the lack of respect he had just shown me with his silly, simple, careless words. I turned the key, pulled it out and threw it at him. I flung open the door and jumped out into the heavy traffic. I cried and banged the roof of the car.

John was standing behind me before I realised he had got out of the car. He put his arms around my shoulders and hugged me tightly. 'We need to keep our heads. We need to be united on this, Jo. Please get back in the car. Let's go home.'

His words made no sense. How could they? I had four weeks left with the man I had spent almost half of my life with. He was going to die, and he was telling *me* we needed to be *united*?

But then, that was my John—the man I had come to know. He was always the calm, reflective one in our relationship. He thought things out. I just lost the head. He always looked at choices. I never thought I had a choice in most things I did. What really scared me now was the prospect of life without him.

John had always believed he would go somewhere better after his life here. I had believed for most of my adult life that there was nothing beyond what I had been given. At that moment, I wanted to believe so badly that there *was* something beyond the word 'goodbye', something that might give me a lasting connection to the man who had been my cornerstone for over twenty years.

We sat together on the double armchair that night. It was something we hadn't done for years. The fire crackled with damp wood and coals. The soft lamp in the corner gave off just enough light for both of us to look at photos. I was glad we had taken the shots on the few holidays we had gone on together over the years. I wished at that moment we had gone on more, that we had travelled the world together.

Instead we had become like most middle-aged couples. We assumed things, took each other for granted and lost sight of what it meant to be best friends. We felt uneasy sitting so close together. Even though I knew our time together was limited to weeks now, the touch of his body so near to me made me uneasy. I longed for closeness to this man, but we had become settled, on our own in our own little worlds. I wanted to be in his arms and to feel loved. I knew he loved me. And I hoped he knew how much I loved him. But it had become easier just to assume he knew.

'Let's go somewhere,' I said nervously. It meant nothing to me. It felt like an unexpected cough that had interrupted a cosy silence.

'Like . . . where?' John sighed. 'When?'

He was telling me there wasn't enough time.

'Remember how you always wanted to visit the Great Barrier Reef? And Times Square? We could go to New York for a long weekend.'

What a stupid line of talk, I remember thinking. But it was better than the silence and the old photos, token gestures of holidays we had gone on because we had become bored with each other at home. None of that mattered any more.

5

'I'd love a dog,' he said softly. Then he smiled.

His words caught me completely off-side. I remembered him telling me that his dog had been killed when he was fourteen. He said it was the worst thing that had ever happened to him. It took him years to get over it.

I hated pets. I had a phobia about cats and another about horses. My first thought was what would I do with the dog when John was gone. 'Where will we get a dog?' I asked.

'The local pound, I suppose. You can give it back later . . . if you don't like it.'

I wasn't even listening to what he was saying. I was nodding and nodding again harder. 'Yes, yes, of course,' I insisted lovingly. 'First thing in the morning, we'll go. And you can pick . . .' I started to cry. It felt like I was talking to a child. I was trying to cheer him up in the light of something neither of us could explain properly or handle as well as we might have thought we could.

3

John spent most of the following day lying on the couch. He stayed in his pyjamas, under the duvet. He looked very tired. His eyes moved between the television and the French doors that opened out onto a small veranda.

It was the start of spring. Small birds sometimes pecked on the kitchen window. They picked at the nuts that he had left out carefully in the home-made wooden bird-house.

'The garden is getting its life back,' he said softly. He pointed to the small chestnut tree at the bottom of the garden. 'Look at the buds,' he said with the wonder of a small child.

I was always fascinated by the way John looked at nature with such raw energy and excitement. It was as if every living plant, each small green fleck, took on a real life of its own. It was as if it acquired a soul when it came into being. Our chestnut tree was no exception. He seemed to look beneath the surface of everything that breathed and drank to stay alive. And he always saw something much deeper, more beautiful and everlasting. And yet, after twenty years of living together, I had never been able to share his raw connection with life and nature. It was a part of him that I felt excluded me. What I didn't realise until midday that day was that I had been excluding *myself* all along.

Shortly after eleven, John complained of feeling sick. He told me the pain was so bad that he could not get comfortable on the chair any more. He had taken his painkillers at eight. He wasn't due another dose of morphine until two. I wanted to give him an extra dose but he waved his hand and forced a smile.

'Will I help you up to bed?'

He shook his head and held his

stomach.

'Will I get the doctor?' I asked nervously.

'No.'

He was in agony. He gritted his teeth and squeezed his eyes closed. His fists formed a knot around his tummy. I felt helpless, as if I was going to cry.

The sound of a car screeching to a halt and a loud howl made me jump. We could hear the piercing yelp of an animal from the street outside. I ran to the front door.

No sooner had I opened it than a white, shaggy dog ran in between my legs, past the staircase and into the sitting-room where John was lying.

I closed the door quickly in case a second dog might follow. Perhaps there had been two of them fighting. I heard a car drive away at speed. I hurried into the sitting-room to find the shaggy dog crouched across John's legs, whimpering and shaking.

'Out!' I shouted.

The frightened dog crouched even lower, shivering and yelping. Her left leg was bleeding. She licked the wound and stuck her head into the crook of John's arm.

'Leave her, Jo. She'll be OK. Let her just catch her breath,' John said softly. He stroked the back of the dog's head.

I watched as John whispered to the dog. He smiled as the dog looked up at him.

'Here, come and pat her,' he said to me.

I shrugged my shoulders. 'What if she bites?'

John smiled. 'Of course she won't bite you. She has just been knocked down. She needs to be loved, not thrown out. Get me a bowl of water and a clean towel. We'll tidy her up a bit.' He felt the dog's leg gently. The animal whimpered and crouched again. 'She can still move her leg. I don't think she's too badly hurt.'

4

Later that day I called the pound. I asked them if they were missing a white, shaggy dog. They said they were. She had escaped while being fed. They asked if we wanted them to come and collect her. John waved his arm from left to right. It was a very clear 'no thanks, we're keeping her.'

And so, in the days and weeks leading up to my husband's death, we adopted a stray dog and fell head over heels in love—not just with her, but also with each other.

Within a week of taking in 'the dog from Death Row', as John had christened her, strange things began to happen in our lives and around the house. John needed less sleep. He was managing on lower doses of morphine, which he didn't need so often.

On the eighth day after the dog's arrival, he asked me if I would like to walk in the park beside our house. Our doctor had warned me that John was not to walk outdoors because of the risk of catching a chest infection. This, I was told, could kill him. John insisted that, whether or not I chose to come with him, he was going.

And so, holding hands, with the dog on a brand new lead, we walked in the afternoon spring sunshine in a quiet part of the park. We chatted about old times. We laughed and squeezed each other's arms like young lovers. It was something we hadn't made time for in a very long time.

We spoke about the weekend we visited Paris to celebrate our first wedding anniversary. We talked about the weekend in Prague we had won in a pub raffle some years before and how we had promised each other we would go back some day. And we laughed.

We laughed at how the dog chased a small hare but couldn't catch it. I watched John throw a large stick and shout to her, 'Fetch!' I couldn't help wondering where he had got this new strength from in just a few days. I had expected that he might need my help getting from the bed to the couch in a matter of those same days. Something was happening— something I couldn't understand.

Another thing occurred within the same few days. Our 'strange' neighbours, as John liked to call them, called to say hello. This might not seem unusual until you consider that they hadn't spoken to us for almost three years! They blamed the sudden halt in our friendship on John's habit of playing Chopin waltzes late into the night. Yet we never once complained about their son's habit of testing his motorbike's engine in their garden shed in the early hours of the morning. We'd built a wall between the two gardens.

They felt that this was a personal slur against them.

In recent days they had heard the dog barking and playing and two people laughing in the back garden. They heard the sound of Chopin filling our home for the first time in years. They admitted that days and nights of curiosity had got the better of them. They called to see if there was room in our lives again for two old friends. And there was.

I didn't like John standing at the garden gate, yelling 'Get back here, you pup!' down the street at the top of his voice. So we needed to agree on a name for the dog. We finally settled on 'Sonny'.

We walked her twice a day, usually in the park. Or, to be honest, she walked us. I marvelled even more now at John's level of energy. He was able to stand straight. And he strode when he walked instead of hobbling from room to room. He slept soundly at night instead of twisting and turning, dreaming and waking.

The doctors were amazed. All they could do was smile and shake their heads. John became absorbed in the life of 'my Sonny', as he called her. And I became absorbed in the life of a man I realised I was only starting to get to know.

5

We met in the most unlikely way. It was on a freezing cold evening in the multi-storey car-park at Dublin airport. I was returning from London, having stayed with my brother for a weekend. After paying my parking fee, I realised I had forgotten where I had parked my car. I wandered for over an hour, searching for a blue Fiesta. I went in and out of parking bays, sure that my car would be around the next corner. It wasn't. I was frozen and close to tears when I heard his voice.

'Are you lost?'

It was a soft, warm voice, filled with concern and a slight touch of amusement. I looked around and stepped out of the glare of his headlights to put a face to the voice. 'Yes, I suppose I am,' I said cautiously.

'Get in and I'll help you find your car.' He pushed open the passenger door. 'What are we looking for?'

I was slightly put off by his casual familiarity. But I was so cold and fed up by then I wouldn't have cared if he were a convicted axe-murderer. We drove around for half an hour and eventually found my Fiesta. By then we knew more about each other than most people find out in a month. *And* he had asked me out.

He was forty-five, he told me—ten years older than I was—and divorced. He was a painter and a musician. He divided his loyalties depending on which was making the most money at the time.

Looking back, I realise I fell in love with John before his rear window had had time to defrost. I felt close to him, important and wanted. He sounded interested in me. He was dying to know all about me, and I loved telling him.

These were feelings I had never

had—feelings that my own marriage had convinced me I never would have. I told him I had been married to a violent bastard who treated me like a doormat for ten years. He had beaten me often and told people he hated me. I divorced at thirty and closed the chapter entitled 'Men' in my book of life. I could do without them, I told myself.

Life was so much better spent alone or with girlfriends. Ask me why and I could have given you twenty reasons. Ask me to describe my perfect man and I would have laughed at the very idea.

Then I lost my car and I met John.

Within two weeks we had moved in together. Because he worked from home a lot we were almost always with each other. But things changed quite quickly. Looking back now, I know my biggest fear was losing him. To what, or to whom, I don't know. I just had this feeling, almost all of the time, that this big, cuddly man was too good for me. I wanted to be with him always. I went to exhibitions and galleries and music festivals as often as I could with him, even though he was always working. I usually sat by the stage if he was playing, or joined the small curious crowds and wandered around if he was displaying his paintings. I needed to see him, out of the corner of my eye, if I was to know that he was still mine.

My friends told me I was mad. They told me no man was worth that effort. But John was worth it and more. So much so that, in the end, I lost contact with many of my old, trusted friends.

I loved him more than life itself. *And* we had only known each other for two months. We celebrated our third month together by dining at Toreador, one of our favourite restaurants. John proposed and placed the most exquisite ring on my finger. I still savour the sound of the word 'yes', which I said from such a depth of love and gratitude.

The man of my dreams had asked me to marry him, and I would. For the first time in years my life felt as if it had a purpose: a beginning and middle. My problem was I still could not stop thinking about all the possible 'ends' that might be waiting for me.

I lived my life through disappointments but carried a cross like a crusader who had returned from the wars. As long as I could recall the bad times I'd survived I felt strong. My problem was that all I could see ahead were more bad times. I suppose it came from familiarity: if you kick a dog hard and often enough, the animal will begin to expect more kicks. It will come to believe that this is what life is all about. That's why a badly treated dog will often run away from the owner who begins to treat it kindly.

Unfortunately my strange behaviour caused a rift between us. While we stayed married, we became strangers under our shared roof. John did his painting in the attic, tuned his mandolin in the drawing-room, while I continued my job as a web-design consultant. We worked from different rooms. Our work kept us distracted, away from having to answer the questions we both knew the other one was silently asking.

The busier I became, the less insecure I felt about John. The busier he was, the less he felt he had to reassure me that he really did love me. I knew he loved me but I suppose I never felt he loved me the way I wanted.

I didn't go to as many of his gigs or exhibitions. So I didn't have to think about the women who would watch him dreamily as he sang their favourite songs, or him explaining to the art-loving women about his brush strokes and colour blends.

It wasn't jealousy, nor was it insecurity, I believe. I really know that now. It was disbelief on my part that such an amazing man could just walk into my life and stay.

6

Sonny came to love Chopin and howled out to the catchy piano melodies late into the afternoon. John sat in the open French doors, his scarf tucked in under a heavy pullover, painting a scene unfolding in our back garden.

A nest of bird eggs had been hatching over a couple of days in the softening spring climate. Six grey wagtails chirped noisily, non-stop, for their mother to bring back worms and crumbs, and seeds and bits, to nourish them.

The noise drove Sonny mad, so John had to turn the stereo up and drown the chirping with the sound of the solo piano. We must have had the only dog in the world that knew all of Chopin's waltzes almost intimately!

I had become worried about John,

24

about his lack of concern for draughts and soakings from spring showers and late nights, and his lack of dietary control. He was even forgetting to take his medicine when he was meant to. But he just laughed and shouted at Sonny.

His specialist phoned one evening. John had gone out to collect new strings for his mandolin. It was the evening I grew to dislike this doctor for his ruthless lack of humanity. This man, having listened to me regaling him about the new dog we had adopted, and the new man I had found as a result, just laughed.

He said, 'Don't be getting your hopes up.'

I was shocked and felt angry. 'Explain what you mean by that,' I said.

He took a deep breath. 'Jo, I've been dealing with cases like John's for almost fifteen years now. He's nothing special. Obviously every case is different. John is simply outliving our expectations. A change of season, improved weather, longer days, more daylight—all these things can lead to greater hopes and beliefs that outcomes will be different. The body responds by adding an extra month or two. That's all.' He chuckled again, as if trying to soften his tone. 'It's certainly not your dog that's helping your husband to live longer. If it is then I want to be Doctor Doolittle!'

I threw the phone down as I heard the key in the front door.

Sonny bounded into the sitting-room and dived onto the good couch. John strode in behind her. 'Who was that?' he asked.

'The hospital.'

'What did they want?'

'Just to know how you're getting on.'

'And what did you tell them?' He smiled and sat down and stroked Sonny's head.

'I told them you were doing

26

fantastic, that you had even surprised yourself.'

John grinned and winked at me. It had been years since we had winked at each other. 'I'll show them,' he said cheekily.

'You have an appointment next Thursday,' I said reluctantly. I didn't want my John going anywhere near the hospital. He was coping beautifully. Anything they were going to tell him now he didn't need to know. He should have died five months ago if their 'rough guess' had been right, but he didn't.

He was fitter and healthier and more positive now than I had ever seen him. He ate heartily, sang his favourite songs and even offered to iron the clothes for me. (We had a joke in our house that we had a 'magic chair' in the kitchen. Since neither of us liked ironing, we just left bundles of clothes on the magic chair in the hope that the other one would iron them.)

John started to do odd jobs around the house. He replaced old light fittings and painted the bathroom the shade of lavender he knew I loved. And, that night the consultant rang, we made love—something neither of us had suggested doing for a long time. That night raised both of us to a new level of love and connection, the likes of which I can't ever recall.

The strange truth for me was that the reason for his new lease of life, and for our new life together, was sitting on the armchair beside him gasping for water. This dog had not only extended my husband's life, but also put the magic back into our friendship as a couple.

7

The visit did not go well. John's specialist sat stony-faced. There were charts and a pad sitting in front of him. 'Still no change, it would appear, John.' He sat still in his starched white coat, his hands almost in prayer, his fingertips stroking his chin. He wanted to hear John's reaction.

John laughed in disbelief. 'But I'm putting on weight. One stone, three pounds in four months! Surely that's a sign that I'm doing really well?'

The doctor shook his head and checked the first chart. 'But this chart clearly shows there's no change.' He pointed to a shadow on the x-ray. It's still there . . . and it's getting bigger.'

John swallowed hard and squeezed my hand.

The doctor picked up a second

chart with pieces of paper attached to one corner. He waited for a minute, as if to make sure he was certain. He cleared his throat. 'Actually the tests we did two weeks ago show that it's spreading, I'm afraid.' It was all he said.

John stood up slowly, pulling me with him as he walked sideways to the door. He nodded at the doctor and we left. The car was quiet all the way home. Usually John would play a tape of Chopin for Sonny, and our white shaggy dog would howl along and stick her head out the back window and bark. Today she just slouched on the back seat. John sat beside me and stared out the window. Sometimes he sighed, with the aimless intent of someone who seemed to have given up hope.

John went upstairs and got into bed, just like he used to when he had been first diagnosed. He was turned to the wall, asleep, when I checked on him.

Sonny lay under the kitchen table while it got dark outside.

I sat alone in the drawing-room of our house that night, late into the night. And I wondered what it would be like to be really alone. What must it be like not to have the one you love call your name, or touch you and kiss you and let you know how loved and wanted you really are?

I had never been a very spiritual person, but I knew something was changing in recent weeks and months. Now, in the silence of the house, I could feel a presence fill the room around me.

Before all this I had been used to living a single life within a relationship with a man I loved. Each of us did our own thing, but we relied on each other for those little moments we needed to be connected for. Now everything each of us did was completely dependent on how the outcome would affect the other. Now I was living half of another's

31

life, and he had become an inseparable half of everything I was.

But that could not happen without the presence of something so much greater that kept the connection between the two of us alive. And we felt connected, whether we were making love, or together in the park holding hands, or at opposite ends of a room, or on opposite sides of the world.

8

I checked my watch. It was after four o'clock in the morning. I'd fallen fast asleep. Sonny was stretched across my lap. I gently patted her back and scratched her head the way John did, knowing she liked it.

This dog was amazing in so many ways. Whatever we had done for her, I was starting to believe that she had completely turned our lives around and put them together again. I hated to think about where John might be now if it hadn't been for the gale-force energy she had breathed into our lives. And in doing so, she had made me think about my life with John and stretched my spirit to get closer to his.

I'd lit a candle and placed it on the coffee table close to the mantelpiece. It gave off a soft glow, and its flame flickered and danced against the wall above the fireplace. It lit up a painting of a bridge in Paris where John had sat for hours one afternoon, sketching and colouring until he was happy with its likeness.

We sat together, dog and human, listening to the songs of George Benson. 'The Greatest Love of All'. It was one of my favourite songs. I stroked her long, matted ears and she nestled into my tummy. She was like a small child—helpless in many ways, but bold and quick in others. While I listened to the songs of my youth I found myself talking to this beautiful animal in a way I'd never have believed I would. 'I love you,' I told her.

She stretched up and licked my face.

'Thank you for what you have done for our John. I really think we might have lost him a good while back if it hadn't been for you coming into our lives.'

She watched me with a gentle,

attentive look. It seemed to tell me this dog was more clever than I'd given her credit for. It almost seemed at one point as if she wanted to respond in words. It was as if she was pushing herself to say something in reply to me.

'You know, I think we're going to have to say goodbye to John very soon,' I said gently, as if not wanting to hurt the dog's feelings. But I needed to say it to someone. I needed badly to bring this hurtful fact into the open so I could feel like I had admitted the truth to myself. Then it occurred to me that I was talking to a four-legged animal like I would my best friend.

This pet of ours couldn't talk, never mind fully understand the feelings behind the things I was telling her. Yet she *was* like a best friend. She felt like someone I could talk to when my *real* best friend was too ill to listen. She whined softly. It made me tremble. She *did* know what I was saying to her. She could feel the distress in my voice. She shivered a little and put her head back down on my stomach.

We fell asleep together as the candle flickered less and eventually died.

Bright sunshine was streaming through the crack in the net curtains when I opened my eyes. The radio was playing in the kitchen, and the music and DJ filled the house with energy. It felt early but I knew it had to be later. It must have been after five when I fell asleep. A blanket covered me. I could smell sausages and black pudding and hear the fresh, sizzling sound of a fry. It was a breakfast I hadn't tasted for years. Sonny's barking echoed around our small back garden. She was warning the birds they were on someone else's patch.

John pushed open the door. He was carrying a tray. On it was a full Irish, a pot of tea, four slices of toast and butter and marmalade.

'I would have done that for you,' I said with thanks.

'I wanted to make it for you. I haven't done it in years.'

I could hear sadness in his voice. We both knew what he meant. It was something he wanted to do because he wouldn't be able to for much longer. I fought back the tears and reached for his hand. 'Thank you.'

9

In the days and weeks that followed, Sonny turned our small house into a warm, loving, welcoming home. Her barking and occasional escape out the front door made the children on our street quite curious. They would return Sonny and stand at the front door and chat to me.

It was the first time since we had moved here that I chatted with our other neighbours. It was one of those streets where people kept very much to themselves. This had distressed me since John became ill. I wondered what I would do if I woke in the night and he needed urgent help.

The children called every day and took it in turns to walk Sonny on her lead in the park beside our house. I told them I couldn't get out as often as I would have liked because my husband was very ill. I told them I needed to stay with him as much as I could. Three of them called at the same time every day—a little girl with curly blonde hair and two small boys. They would ask if I needed anything from the local shops. Soon I had a small shopping list ready for them when they called.

Within days I had a call from one of their parents, a lovely woman who was worried that her daughter might be annoying us by calling too often. I assured her she wasn't. I explained to her that John had cancer. The woman told me her name was Nancy. Soon we were close friends. She cooked meals, put out bins and tidied rooms if I needed her help. Word was getting around. Days later others were calling, asking if I needed anything, if they could sit with John while I took a break. Before long I realised I had a small group of new friends who genuinely were concerned for both of us.

Once again it was all down to Sonny. She had worked her way into the lives of the children. In turn, their parents had come and found me just when I needed people badly.

I had always believed I could do everything on my own. I believed it was not necessary to rely on others to get on in life. John had become my rock of support. He was there when I needed a second opinion. I could just look around and know that he was there for me.

Now I know that was just a serious case of taking someone else for granted. I know that simply because I felt that John loved me, I thought I could assume things about our relationship. It never occurred to me that this man would not be there forever. I always thought I would die before him. It was what I would have wanted, but maybe that's just an excuse, a cop-out.

The longer a relationship endures the easier it becomes to assume that it will continue. The last thing I was expecting was that John would die. I often told myself that he might come home some day and tell me he had met someone else. I think it would have been painfully difficult to hear him say those words. But it would have been easier than to hear a man in a white coat tell me stone-cold that my partner was going to die on me.

10

One day I was walking Sonny in the park. It was fresh and windy but the sun shone. Nancy had offered to sit with John while he had his afternoon nap. His energy levels were still good over the last couple of weeks. But I had detected a definite change. His appetite was poorly again and he wasn't sleeping well. I boosted my hopes by reminding myself that at least the pain wasn't as bad as it had been. He would sleep most afternoons from three to five. I would use the time to get some fresh air, to walk and to put things in my head into perspective.

Sonny loved the park, chasing squirrels and barking at birds and bicycles. I was amazed at how quickly she could suddenly tear after something she'd heard rustling in the ditches and the rough hedges. She would stop, dead still, then bark and break into a wild sprint.

But then, just as I had fixed her in my sight in the distance, she was gone. She had vanished. I looked around, searched everywhere. I listened for her barking and the way she would howl at small animals she might hear or see in the undergrowth. But there were no sounds. There was no familiar barking, just the noise of the traffic and the occasional blast of wind in the trees that surrounded me as I searched for her without luck.

I cried all the way home and cursed God for messing things up so nicely. I suddenly became aware again of how brittle and uncertain our lives had become. It was as if Sonny had bonded our existence with glue. It felt like she had patched things up for us during a period of fear and the unknown. She added simplicity to our lives that had helped us to deal with the horrible prospects that lay ahead. I realised that whenever Sonny wasn't close to me, the awful truth about John's health and the few weeks I had left with him became all too painful.

And what would I tell John? He'd always said, 'Keep her on the lead.' But I couldn't in the park. It didn't seem fair. She needed to be released. She needed to do what the other dogs loved to do. Anyway she had become so strong she could dislocate my shoulder if I tried to hold on to her. She needed to run unleashed for the hour she was free.

I tried to imagine a variety of excuses, but there were none. I dreaded the moment I would have to tell him. He was waiting for me inside the door when I arrived home.

His reaction shocked me. He smiled and said, 'She'll be back.' He hugged me tightly.

'But what if she's been taken by someone?' I asked in disbelief.

He shook his head. 'I'll bet you

she'll be back here within a few hours.'

I wanted to ask how he could be so sure, but I didn't. I just prayed and hoped he would be right. I called the local police station. They told me there was little they could do. I rang the pound. They told me they would watch out for her. They knew her and would call if anyone sighted her.

I wrote out small notices, placed them in local shop windows and waited for it to become dark. And then I became very upset at the thought of my little baby out there on her own on the cold streets, hungry and lost. She really had become the centre of our lives.

'She'll be back tomorrow,' John kept saying as he coaxed me to eat something that night.

And he was right. The following afternoon Sonny came home.

The young boy wouldn't give his name. He was about fourteen, tall, dark-haired and familiar looking, although I couldn't place him. He smiled, out of breath. He seemed in a hurry. He struggled to keep Sonny in his arms. As soon as I opened the door, the dog jumped down and shot in past me, landing on John's lap with a thump.

'Where did you find her?' I asked him.

'She ran into our back garden and barked. I heard a screech. She must have run out on the road in front of a car. Lucky for her she didn't get knocked down. I knew she was Sonny because I saw my friends taking her to the shop last week.'

I took some coins out of my pocket and handed them to him. He looked with wide-open eyes, then shook his head. 'No really,' he insisted, 'it's OK. Thank you.' He backed away, closed the garden gate and was gone. I went after him but he had turned the corner by the time I'd reached the street.

All the things I never thought

would happen were starting to unfold. My sister, whom I hadn't spoken to since I'd got married, phoned me. Penny apologised for not getting in touch. We'd had a terrible row because I hadn't asked her to be my bridesmaid. We'd married in Rome. I explained we couldn't afford a big wedding but she took it personally and didn't talk to me until that afternoon that Sonny came home.

She had heard from one of my neighbours that John was ill. She cried when I told her how sick he really was. She promised to call the following weekend and spend some time with us.

'Jo, I'm really sorry. This should never have happened. I miss you,' she said tearfully.

'It's OK. I've missed you too, for so long,' I replied. I put the phone down and felt a huge sense of relief and a surge of comfort. Now I was going to have my big sister back in my life—someone I knew would look out for me and look after me.

11

As the days became longer and grew warmer, our time together was growing shorter. John slept more during the day but often lay awake for hours at night. The doctor suggested it might be better for both of us to sleep in separate beds. That way John might be more comfortable and I would enjoy longer spells of sleep.

We both agreed this would not happen. We needed to be as close as we could to each other. So we slept beside each other, holding hands, clinging to each other's necks or shoulders, or stroking each other's cheeks. Despite the discomfort and pain he was clearly suffering, he never once complained. He would just squeeze my hand and force a small, short smile. I had started to tell John I loved him at every available opportunity. And he said the same to me.

Sonny lay across the end of the bed all the time now. It was as if she was keeping watch, waiting for a moment that we both seemed to know was becoming closer by the hour.

The doctor told me it would only be a matter of days now. John asked him to stop giving him pain-killing injections. They relieved the pain but took away his sense of awareness and brought on a sickening sleep that took him hours to wake up from.

And so my John was acutely aware of what was going on around him, but also in acute pain from a disease that was quickly claiming him.

One night I lulled him to sleep, humming a few lines from one of his favourite Chopin waltzes. His breathing was heavy and wheezy, so I rubbed his back as he lay peacefully on his side. Once I knew he was sleeping, I patted Sonny on the head and lay back on the bed and closed my eyes.

I dreamed of the small church in Rome, Our Lady of the Vines, and the beautiful day we had been given for our secret wedding. There was a smell of lavender and honey melon in the air. The peacefulness of the small churchyard in the foothills above the city took my breath away. We'd planned it quickly, with no fuss and no guests. A friend of John's acted as our witness. The priest blessed our vows in a twenty-minute ceremony overlooking the River Tiber.

We stayed on for a week, in a beautiful chateau that Eric, John's friend, had organised for us. We lazed together during the warm days, sampling local wines and eating home-baked, piping-hot lasagne. And we were so deeply in love with each other that words were not easy to find to describe the intensely wonderful feelings we had for each other.

We marvelled at the unspoilt beauty of the mountains. The lush greenery seemed more intense and memorable because we were looking at it through each other's eyes. And every time John told me he loved me, he fired up my soul to a new level. I needed him, breathed in every minute we spent together that week. I missed him terribly whenever he went to make a phone call or when Eric stole him away for an hour.

And how is it that the years in between can turn something so precious and love-made into a casual friendship that runs skin deep? How can such intense feelings become distant memories? How could my man and I forget what it was like to feel weak in the presence of such beauty?

I opened my eyes. I remembered it with the same intensity. I realised that I had been given another chance with this amazing man. We had at our fingertips the emotions we felt all those years ago. A dog had caused us to look at each other closely and to fall in love again. We were falling in love at a special time. It was a period where there was no room for doubt, or second opinions, or fear, or questions.

I couldn't help thinking about the petty tiffs and the silly rows we had built up like walls over the years, usually because one of us wasn't getting what we wanted, what we demanded. And these arguments often stemmed from my refusal to accept that John had a say, not just in his life, but also in mine.

Yet these petty disputes never featured during those times when a sense of love and connection dominated our lives. When we got close-up and honest with each other, there was a depth of understanding that became the mainstay of our relationship. I'd missed that deep sense of belonging for so long.

Now—thanks to a stray dog that ran past me at my front door and made our home her home—I had that love and caring back in my heart and back in my life for a second time.

12

The room was warm. In the distance I could hear the early milk-float. Birds were chirping in the trees at the bottom of the garden. Dawn was breaking. It startled me. I must have slept for hours. Jesus! What if John had been calling my name?

I sat up quickly and looked at the small alarm clock on the bedside table. It was after five. I'd slept for three hours. I checked my man and I froze. He was lying perfectly still. Something inside told me not to panic. He seemed slumped on his side, his arm hanging over the edge of the bed, silent and still.

I could feel my heart speed up. The tears began to well in my eyes. I placed my hand over my mouth as I whispered his name. 'John . . . *John*!' I said louder.

He didn't answer.

I jumped out of bed and tried to think of what I had to do. 'Don't do this, John. Please don't go!' I remember saying as I ran around to his side of the bed. I knelt beside him and shook his arm. He didn't move. His eyes were barely open. He had a peaceful look on his face. There was no pain any more. He didn't seem bothered by how sick he had been getting in recent weeks. He looked resigned now.

Tears streamed down my face as I stroked his hair and whispered, 'I love you with all my heart and all my life.' Normally he would react by smiling first and then hugging me and repeating the words back. But that morning, my John was beyond telling me anything in the earthly sense.

I hugged him and watched as Sonny edged forward cautiously and licked John's ear. She whimpered and sat to one side as I tried to make John more comfortable in the bed.

He was heavier than usual, despite the way the disease had ravaged him and, lately, caused him to lose five stone in weight.

I felt his forehead. The clammy dampness that I'd felt for weeks had been replaced now with cooler, softer skin. I placed my ear to his nose and listened for a breath. I gently pressed his chest, hoping for a small heartbeat. I placed a pillow behind him and propped his head forward so I could hold him in my arms.

I was too late.

I phoned the pound later that afternoon to tell them Sonny had gone missing again. I told the caring voice on the phone that my husband had died. I didn't have a chance to look for my dog because I had been so busy with people calling and plans to be made. I'd left the side gate open and she must have slipped out. I remembered John's words. 'She'll be back in a few hours.' And I asked

John to bring her back to me.

I spent that day asking John to please come back too. I wandered in and out of the bedroom where he had lain for weeks. The bed was empty now, but the house was filled with something I found hard to describe. It was something—a sense of warm spirit—I felt my husband had left behind to help me through the grief and the sheer sense of loss. It's only now, when I look back on the never-ending hours of those first few days, that I realise he was carrying me. It felt like he was saying to me, 'Thank you for the weeks and months *you* carried *me*.'

Neighbours called on and off for a couple of weeks. The friendships I had built up over the time leading up to John's death became my support. The pain of loss, and the loneliness that comes with it, were strangely kept at bay by the empathy and outpouring of emotion that came with the hugs and soft words of encouragement and handshakes. I felt like I was floating, unsure of what was going on and what I could expect to happen next.

While the adults chatted kindly and poured me more drinks, the children searched for Sonny. Notices were hung in shop windows again. The police were contacted and I waited. But she didn't come home.

13

Part of me wanted them all to go home, to stop calling to see if I was 'doing fine'. But a deeper part of me didn't want to be alone in this house now. My husband was gone and my dog had vanished—all in the same breath, it felt.

My life was on hold it seemed. I needed answers to questions. I prayed that I might be sent a sign to let me know that John was fine, that he was beyond the awful pain and torment of the last few months. I wanted to be sure that he hadn't gone somewhere where he suffered alone and the pain grew worse. But whom was I praying to?

It made no sense. My world felt utterly empty now, and the idea of praying to someone I couldn't see, to a God I'd never really believed in, seemed like a daft notion. If there really was a God—I must confess I didn't believe there was—then why had he left me without both husband and dog? I tried to imagine the kind of support Sonny might have been to me in the days and weeks after John's death. How could a loving and kind God deprive me so harshly? It made no sense to me. I started to spend hours of each new, awful day in bed with the curtains closed.

The death of someone so loved creates such chaos in one's life that it's almost too hard to explain and too painful to search for words that might explain it.

It was only after John's death that I began to realise the personal space he occupied in my life, in my mind and in my soul. I had always been the cynical one in our house. 'Of course there's no such thing as life after death!' I would say whenever John got into one of his deep-thinking moods. He had always told me he wasn't afraid of dying. I had asked him to stop being so morbid. It was because I was terrified of the idea of death, because I couldn't see beyond its final moments.

In the weeks after his death I cried for him. I longed for our dog who would have remained a connection between us. I felt so lost that I thought about ending my own life to be with him, if there was such a place to be. My sister Penny begged me to go to the doctor.

'He'll give you something to help you get over this,' she said kindly.

'Help me get over *what*?' I shouted at her.

What exactly did she think I wanted to be helped over? People seem to think it goes away or it gets better after a few weeks. Others think you wake up some morning and decide you've had enough crying: it's time to pick up the pieces and pull yourself together.

I know I felt like that at times in the past when I looked at other people trying to cope with loss that knows no depths.

I asked Penny to go home that evening. She refused. I demanded. She went. It was one of those lowest moments that sometimes defines the most difficult stage of grief, that instantly comes to mind when we look back at something that almost destroyed us.

I decided to go back to bed forever that afternoon. I'd make a cup of tea, add a very large brandy and lie down. I wanted to be alone with nicer thoughts that I'd try to find once the room was dark and life felt shut out.

And then it happened—one of those moments that utterly changes everything you've ever believed in the value of, everything you thought was impossible and terrifying and beyond reason.

14

I was stirring the mug of tea when I caught the spoon in the cuff of my sleeve. The boiling tea spilled across the work-top and down onto the floor, splashing and burning my hand.

I tried to remember where I had put the tube of burn cream I'd kept for cases of emergency. I took the entire contents of the bathroom cabinet out, rooted through presses and checked drawers. John must have taken it and put it somewhere else. I was about to close the bottom kitchen drawer, which was full to the brim with everything from a needle to an anchor, when I spotted it.

It was a bulging cardboard wallet, packed tightly with dozens of old photos. Most of them were colour but some were black and white. It hurt me horribly to think there were some of John and me together down through the years that I hadn't seen for ages. But curiosity got the better of me.

I sat on the armchair, close to the French windows where I'd felt so peaceful in the past. I started to place the photos neatly on the coffee table. Some I recognised easily. Others bore faces I'd forgotten with time. They must have been tucked away at the back of the drawer for ten years. And then I saw it.

It was a strange photo, black and white, worn and ragged around the corners. It must have been thirty years old, at least. Three rows of teenage boys sat neatly for the camera. I studied each row, each face and then . . . I froze. My heart started to pound again, the way it did the moment I woke and realised my husband had gone.

There, in the front row, was a young boy I recognised. He was sitting for the photo and smiling, holding a white shaggy dog. It was the young boy who had called at my hall door the previous week, having found Sonny in his back garden. The dog was identical to my Sonny.

The shock was almost too much. It didn't make any sense to me whatsoever. I felt frightened and slightly sick to think that it might not be a coincidence. But it had to be. This photo was thirty years old. The young boy who called to my door carrying Sonny was no older than fourteen. But the likeness was chilling.

The caption 'Intermediate Junior Football Champions 1971' was printed across the top of the photo along with the name of the school. I studied it again and again for maybe an hour. Each time I picked it up I held it closer. I wanted to find reasons to believe that this boy and his dog were not whom I thought they were.

A few minutes later I had found

the phone number of the college. I hesitated, waiting to think about what I might be told once the phone was answered. What if they didn't have any records? What if they said they couldn't tell me what I needed to know?

The phone rang and rang. Eventually a softly spoken voice out of breath answered. 'Hello, Saint Paul's. Can I help you?' She waited.

I froze. I hung up. And then I called again. 'I hope you can help me. I found an old photo dating back to 1971. I'm trying to identify someone in the shot. Would you have such records?' I waited, feeling the pace of my heart.

'Not right away. But I could call you back, possibly today, with the information. That's if we still have it on record.'

I thanked her and hung up. The silence of the house made my heartbeat sound louder. I tried to relax but couldn't. It occurred to me that I'd forgotten how sore my hand was. It was swollen now, but the excitement and anticipation I felt seemed to drown out the pain.

I was dozing when the phone rang an hour or so later. The college secretary asked to speak to me and told me her name. I held my breath and waited. She told me the young student I had been asking about was called John Duhan. My married name was Duhan. The boy was John, my husband.

I don't remember saying goodbye, or putting the phone down, or finding myself walking in the park in the spring sunshine on a windy afternoon in March. It all seemed just to happen. It made no sense to me at all. But in another way it made sense as to why Sonny had gone within hours of John's death. It gave a whole new meaning to the expression 'A dog is a man's best friend.'

I felt lonely that afternoon, but

lonely in a different way to how I'd been feeling in recent days. I was happy to know that two lifelong friends had been reunited once again and that one of them had come to the aid of the other when he was in his hour of most need. Sonny had rarely left John's side in the short time he had left here. Now I knew why.

I suppose it's a sad story with a happy ending. It makes me realise that I, like so many others, have taken so much for granted during my lifetime.

I always thought I made the rules that determined how I lived. Now I know there's so much more going on than we really pay heed to. If only we could, life would mean so much more. The pain we feel we have to suffer would melt away to be replaced by hope and wonder.

John's death has given way to an understanding and a belief I never thought I would be able to share with anyone—not even in my quietest moments when I talk to myself. Now I know John *is* more than life itself, and just as Sonny was there for him, he is *always* there for me.